THE BIG BOOK OF DC★SUPER FRIENDS

™

By Frank Berrios

 A GOLDEN BOOK • NEW YORK

Copyright © 2015 DC Comics.
DC SUPER FRIENDS and all related characters and elements
are trademarks of and © DC Comics.
WB SHIELD: ™ & © Warner Bros. Entertainment Inc.
(s15)

RHUS34605

randomhousekids.com   ISBN 978-0-553-50773-7 (trade)—ISBN 978-0-553-50774-4 (ebook)   Printed in the United States of America
10 9 8 7 6 5 4 3 2 1

Superman

Superman is one of the most powerful heroes on Earth. He uses his **super-strength** and mighty powers to **protect our world** from super-villains, alien invasions, and natural disasters.

Superman comes from a planet called Krypton.

Earth's yellow sun gives Superman **incredible superpowers**. He can **fly**, **punch** through walls, and even **outrun** high-speed trains!

Powers

- Super-strength
- Invulnerability
- Flight
- Super-speed
- X-ray vision
- Heat vision
- Super-breath
- Super-hearing

Superman is a champion of **truth** and **justice**, and he is always ready to help those in need. He is Earth's **greatest hero**!

LEX CORP

Supergirl

Supergirl is Superman's cousin. She is also a **powerful hero**. She is always ready to lend Superman a helping hand—or give the bad guys a **superpowered punch**!

Like Superman, Supergirl gets her powers from Earth's sun. Don't let her sweet smile fool you—Supergirl is an **unstoppable force** for good!

Powers
- Super-strength
- Flight
- Super-speed
- X-ray vision
- Heat vision
- Super-breath
- Super-hearing

Bizarro is Superman's **imperfect opposite**—he has powers like Superman's, but none of his brains! Instead of heat vision and freeze breath, Bizarro has **freeze vision** and **flame breath**. Thankfully, Bizarro's backward thinking allows the Man of Steel to always gain the upper hand!

Bizarro

Lex Luthor

Lex Luthor is one of Superman's **greatest foes**. He is an evil genius bent on **destroying** the Man of Steel. Lex discovered that a green stone called Kryptonite is the only thing that can hurt Superman. He has created lots of fantastic inventions, but not even a genius like Lex can figure out a way to defeat Superman!

Batman

Talents and Skills

- Olympics-level athlete
- Master of disguise
- Escape artist
- Karate and boxing expert
- Extremely intelligent

Batman is the **protector** and **defender** of Gotham City. He wages a never-ending war on crime. Batman strikes fear in the hearts of evildoers everywhere!

Batman is called the **Dark Knight** because he is the greatest crime fighter of all!

Batman doesn't have superpowers, so he uses his brains and **crime-fighting tools** to bring down the bad guys. He wears a Utility Belt filled with everything he needs to fight crime, such as Batropes, Batarangs, and Bat-Cuffs.

Talents and Skills

- Amazing athlete
- Talented acrobat
- Expert fighter
- Loyal, trustworthy, and honest
- Very smart

When trouble arises, Robin **leaps** into action! Robin, the Boy Wonder, is Batman's **trusted partner**. Super-villains and thugs are no match for the **Dynamic Duo**!

Robin

Robin had to train very hard to become **Batman's partner**. Like
Batman, Robin doesn't have superpowers, so this quick-thinking kid
uses his *amazing acrobatic skills* to stop criminals in their tracks!

Batgirl

Talents and Skills

- Karate expert
- Computer expert
- Amazing athlete
- Highly intelligent

When the Dynamic Duo need help, they call Batgirl! Batgirl is dedicated to **fighting crime**.

Like Batman and Robin, Batgirl wears a gadget-filled **Utility Belt**. Don't be surprised if you see Batgirl leaping, fighting, or swinging through Gotham City!

The Batcave

The Dynamic Duo keep their eyes on criminals from their **secret hideout**, the Batcave. It's packed with everything they need to **solve crimes**.

Batman's high-powered car is called the **Batmobile**. It is super-fast! This **rocket-powered** vehicle has an onboard computer and crime lab, and laser-beam headlights!

The **Batcomputer** is filled with files on all of Batman's greatest foes, such as the Joker, Catwoman, and Croc, to name a few!

No matter what the threat, Batman is ready! He uses his **Batcopter** to take to the skies, and his **Batcycle** to hit the streets. His **Batboat** is the fastest ship on the sea!

Batman's Vehicles

The Joker

The Joker is the clown prince of crime! Batman has battled this **twisted trickster** for years, but every time he drags him off to jail, the Joker finds a way to get free!

Two-Face is a villain with a **one-two punch**! He flips a two-headed coin to decide whether he should commit a crime. The Dynamic Duo are determined to stop Two-Face before he strikes again!

Two-Face

Catwoman

Catwoman is a clever **jewel thief**. Batman and Robin have crossed paths with this black cat many times. The heroes are eager to find her a new home—behind bars!

With **tough leather** skin, Croc is a dangerous villain. He makes his home in the **sewers** beneath Gotham City, waiting for his chance to strike. But he's no match for the Dark Knight!

Wonder Woman

Wonder Woman is a **fearless fighter** for peace and justice! She has super-strength and **super-speed**. She uses them to battle villains of all shapes and sizes.

Wonder Woman is a member of the **Amazons**, a tribe of women who live on the secluded Paradise Island. Wonder Woman uses her **unbreakable** Lasso of Truth to wrap up bad guys. This golden lasso forces villains to tell the truth.

Wonder Woman also wears indestructible silver **bracelets** on each wrist. They can deflect any attack.

Powers and Skills

- Fearless warrior
- Super-strength
- Super-speed
- Extremely intelligent

Cheetah

Wonder Woman and Cheetah have clashed many times. This **mischievous menace** will do anything to get her paws on Wonder Woman's golden lasso!

Using both her brains and her brawn, Wonder Woman has defeated Cheetah at every turn. But the Amazon Princess knows it won't be long before she faces this **feline villain** again!

The Green Lanterns

The Green Lantern Corps is dedicated to **stopping evil** throughout the universe. The Green Lanterns are like **police in space**!

Green Lanterns wear **power rings** that are charged with unlimited emerald **energy**. Their rings allow them to fly, create anything they can imagine, and even protect them as they explore deep space!

The Green Lanterns have **protected Earth** from invading aliens, meteor showers, and more. But there are villains with power rings, too. . . .

Sinestro

Sinestro was once a member of the Green Lantern Corps, but he grew **hungry for more power**.

Now Sinestro wears a yellow ring that is similar to the power rings worn by the Green Lanterns. It creates objects that will help him **destroy** the Green Lantern Corps once and for all!

Atrocitus and Dex-Starr are members of the **evil** Red Lantern Corps. They both wear **red power rings**, but instead of helping people, the Red Lanterns want to **rule the universe**!

Atrocitus & Dex-Starr

The Flash

The Flash is the **Fastest Man Alive**!
The Flash has the power to move at super-speed,
which he uses to fight crime. He is sometimes
called the **Scarlet Speedster**.
He does everything fast—he even enjoys
speed-reading his favorite books!

Bad guys, beware: the Scarlet Speedster can easily avoid punches. He can **outrun** the fastest car, train, or plane—and he rarely gets tired. The Flash is so fast, he can even run straight up a wall!

Powers and Skills

- Super-speed
- Endurance
- Fast thinking
- Top-level athlete

Gorilla Grodd

Gorilla Grodd is a genius with the power to **control** the minds of others. As leader of Gorilla City, Gorilla Grodd would like nothing more than to defeat the **pesky humans** who are destroying the planet.

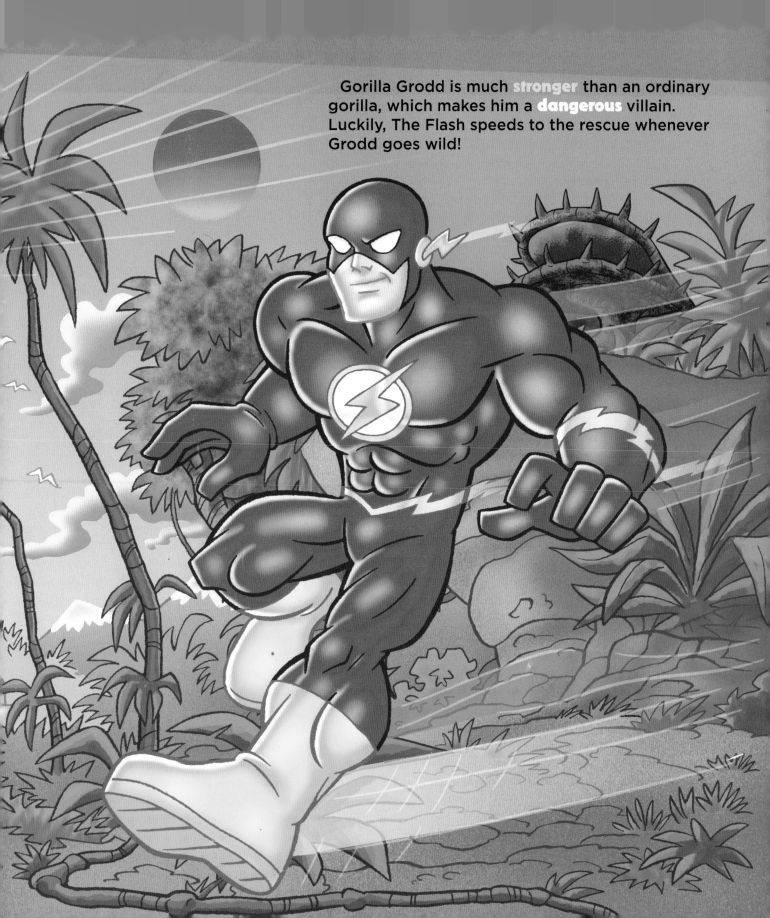

Gorilla Grodd is much **stronger** than an ordinary gorilla, which makes him a **dangerous** villain. Luckily, The Flash speeds to the rescue whenever Grodd goes wild!

Aquaman

Aquaman is an **underwater** super hero who protects Earth's oceans. As King of the Seven Seas, Aquaman has battled modern-day pirates and those who seek to poison the sea. He's a **hero** of the deep!

Powers and Skills

- Can breathe underwater
- Can communicate with sea creatures
- Super-strength
- Fast swimmer
- Extremely intelligent
- Top-level athlete

Black Manta

The villain known as Black Manta uses a powerful **suit of armor** to search the ocean for hidden treasure. His greed has made him one of Aquaman's greatest foes!

Black Manta's costume protects him from the cold waters of the deep. And the lenses in his helmet can fire dangerous laser beams!

Black Manta wants to become the **ruler of the oceans**. He can be stopped by only one person—Aquaman!

Cyborg

Cyborg is half man and **half machine**, but all hero! Cyborg's body has been enhanced with mechanical parts made of reinforced steel and high-tech **computer technology**. His upgrades make him a force to be reckoned with!

Cyborg is more **powerful** than normal humans. His boot jets allow him to fly, and thanks to his **armor**, he can even breathe underwater, just like Aquaman!

Powers and Skills

- Super-strength
- Super-speed
- Flight
- Infrared eye
- Sonic cannon
- Mechanically enhanced body

Hawkman

Hawkman and Hawkgirl are **winged warriors** from a faraway planet called Thanagar. Now these crime fighters **patrol** the skies over Earth!

Powers and Skills

- Flight
- Super-strength
- Super-speed
- Skilled fighters

Hawkgirl

When the Super Friends need help, these heroes never hesitate to **fly** into the fray of a fierce fight!

Unlike Cyborg, Hawkman and Hawkgirl don't like to use modern weapons. They prefer to use weapons from the past, which is why they rarely fly without their trusty **maces**!

Hawkman and Hawkgirl can use their **wings** to fly at great speeds and lift very heavy objects.

Green Arrow

The **hero** known as Green Arrow taught himself how to use a bow and arrow. Now this master **archer** uses his skills to fight crime!

Green Arrow doesn't have superpowers, so he uses a wide variety of **trick arrows** to **stop villains**. He has firecracker arrows and boomerang arrows—and even a boxing-glove arrow that delivers a knockout punch!

Wherever there is greed and corruption,
Green Arrow can be found fighting for **justice**!

These fearless heroes work together to protect the universe from the forces of evil. They are the **Super Friends**!